AF416449

Seduction Lies & Lusts by Krista Toodle

Table of Contents

SEDUCTION, LIES & LUSTS

By Natalie Roberts

Prologue

Woke up so horny, the past 3 days I couldn't resist myself from licking my fingers and rubbing on my clit at least twice each day. But that is no longer enough. I need to feel someone else's lips sucking on my pussy and sliding that hard dick in and out of me. I had a few guys I could call, but I haven't had sex with them recently because I wasn't satisfied by what they did before. I want someone new. I want to have that sex that most of us try to resist, you know that one that gets you wet just from the first meet, when the man is trying to talk his way into some pussy, looking so sexy, and the attraction is so strong that you just want him right then and there. I want something spontaneous!

I have been chatting with a few guys on an online dating site. A few regulars that only went as far as "how was your day?", "what have you been up to?" So I message this one guy named Sylvester that I have been chatting with for about a week, but we haven't met in person yet. I say, "Hey I want to do something adventurous and spontaneous, are you up for it? I want to go to a secluded area in a park where we can get out of the car and have some safe and protected foreplay." Of course he says yes and "meet me in 30 minutes!"

Sylvester is a pretty boy. 6"2', light skinned muscular build and ohhh those green eyes make me quiver. We meet at one of our state parks. When I get out to hug him, he smells so good, I start getting wet right then and there. We find a nice wooded area that appears secluded. Mind you, it is 3 in the afternoon. As we're getting deeper in the woods he's rubbing on my nipples, lifting my dress up, showing all my ass. I'm not wearing panties. My pussy gets so wet. We eventually stop and start kissing. When I reach into his pants and grab his dick, I am pleased by his size and hoping he knows how to hit the right spots. Although I brought protection for some oral foreplay, that is not needed. I am so wet that he just slips the condom on and slides right inside me.

He is hitting it okay, a little turned on and distracted from voices of others nearby, but that doesn't stop us. Still stroking it, he tells me that he'll keep stroking until I cum, but he already came. That is exciting but now I am ready to do it in a bed, so we head back to his place. While I'm following him back to his place and talking to him on the phone, he asks if I am hungry and offers me some dinner that he had cooked. *Nice dick and he can cook*. My panties are getting wet again. He stayed in an apartment near the lake. We chat about how much we love fishing while he fixes my plate. He serves me spaghetti made with turkey meat with added Parmesan cheese, a piece of chicken drumstick and homemade coleslaw. I'm greedy so the combination doesn't bother me at all. The food is delicious!!

After my food settles, he begins to undress me, kiss me, his lips so soft, and his kisses moist and tender. When he puts his lips on my very sensitive nipples, I feel my body tingle from my nipples all the way down to my moist pussy. His touch is amazing, sending chills all over me. We try oral on each other, the safe way, with plastic wrap but that is a FAIL. When I try to suck his dick, the plastic wrap balls up at the tip and we don't use any lubrication so that ends quick. He tries to put the plastic wrap on his tongue so he could lick my pussy but almost chokes because the plastic wrap gets stuck in his throat. Luckily, sucking on my nipples gets me turned on enough to want him to put his dick in me. After putting the condom on, we try doggy style, him on top, then me on top. It's good but I know it's going to take something more for me to cum. Is it the condom, us not really knowing much about each other and trying to figure out what pleases each other, or is it that his stroke is just not that good?

He suggests we lie on our sides as he hits it from the back. OMG that is the best idea ever!! After about 5 strokes, my pussy is soaking wet and the more he strokes the more my body trembles. He finds that spot that makes me squirt, and I am in heaven. Usually when I get to this level of excitement, I start giggling. Now I'm thinking a few more strokes and he'll be cumming too. I AM WRONG!! As he continues to stroke my pussy, every stroke is hitting that spot. Now I'm thinking good thoughts because I'm making up for the past 3 months that I had no sex at all.

After 5 more minutes of continuous stroking, I find myself getting irritated because he hasn't come yet and I am getting tired of cumming back to back. When I tell him I'm ready for him to squirt his cum, his strokes slow down just a bit and I feel more movement from him. After a few more strokes, I look back at him and realize he is recording us on his phone. *Oh Hell No!* I yell, "Stop" and instantly the mood is gone! I jump up and yell, "Delete that shit. You are not showing my pussy to nobody. I decide who gets to see it, not you!!!" He tries to assure me that it is for his eyes only, but I snatch his phone and delete it myself. Jump in the shower, get dressed and I'm out!!!

Blame it on my job!! When you are an intelligent, outgoing woman that has common sense, but your aura is always sexual, you end up in a lifestyle of seduction. Being a constant tease leads to good fortune in exotic dancing and phone sex, but eventually you give in to temptation. Come join me and see what gets exposed.

1.

What I Do

Usually I don't get that turned on when I'm working, doing phone sex, but a few customers want me to watch porn with them and in between calls I look at trending videos and start teasing myself by rubbing on my pussy, getting it wet and juicy.

Yes, I'm a phone sex operator. I've been doing this for about 10 years now. I've always been the one for conversations and was told that I have a soothing voice. When I was in my late teens, I spent a lot of time on the phone talking and flirting with guys I liked. Being an immature teenager with raging hormones, I would call those 900 numbers and listen to the recordings of ladies moaning and talking about different sex acts they wanted to do. Every now and then I would do prank calls and connect someone on the 3-way with me and those recordings. I was calling those 900 numbers so often that I knew the script word for word.

		The majority of my male friends said that I have a sexy voice and even wanted me to have phone sex with them. As I got older, I mean I thought about it, but I didn't think they still did that being the free porn was becoming really popular. So one day I googled "How To Be a Phone Sex Operator" and it led me to a lot of sexy jobs. Modeling, phone sex, video and web cams were the most popular positions offered. I was a little hesitant to apply for these type of jobs, but being a single mother, in my early twenties, with a son, and my health slowly starting to fail due to having lupus, I needed to find a way to bring in a steady income. I've always dreamed of being a CEO of a business or company because I want to be the boss. I was getting tired of people telling me what to do. Jobs telling me to come in early, stay late, must attend a mandatory meeting that interfered with what I needed to do during my time off. I tried many "work from home" opportunities that turned out to be pyramid schemes. After doing a lot of research, I did find one type of business that was recession proof, The Sex Industry. Whether it be prostitution, exotic dancers, phone sex operators or nude web cams, money is always being spent here.

		I applied to several different companies and had interviews with about 3 of them. I had to read a script in my sexiest voice and answer questions that seemed to test my open-mindedness. The first company I worked with was the worst. I had to chat in a chat room and try to convince guys to call me. That's called trolling. A lot of times when they did call, they were already close to cumming and for the most part they only wanted to hear me moaning. Those calls would always be very short. Although I didn't have to hear him breathing hard and stroking his cock (white men call them cocks, black men call them dicks) real fast with lotion on it for a long time, more time equals more money. I started when my son was in middle school. I worked out of my basement, the night shift from 11 pm to 7 am while my son was asleep, and I would go to sleep while he was in school.

My character on the phone was a 23-year-old white female who lived in Tennessee. After a while, I would get regular callers, and sometimes we would talk about other things besides sex. I had this one regular caller named John that lived in Mississippi. He was a white man in his 70's and the CEO of a huge company. We would talk about how our day went and catching up on things since the last time we talked. We would spend about 2 hours on the phone. I would tell him about my money struggles, and he would motivate me to never give up on my dreams. The last twenty minutes of the call, he would talk about how he wishes he was with me right then and holding, kissing, and caressing on me. It was against the rules for us to give out any personal information. No real names, phone numbers, emails, or anything, but I broke that rule with John when he offered to Western Union me some money to help with my struggles. I was a little concerned about giving out my address and real name but considering that he was in his mid-70's and lived in Mississippi, I figured it was a slim chance of him showing up on my doorstep. Anyway, he would be shocked to see a 35-year-old (this was 10 years ago), short and petite black woman wearing glasses.

Two days after I gave him my information, he called my home phone and told me he sent me some money to pay some bills and enjoy a night out. I asked him how much he sent me and when he told me $2500.00, I immediately started getting so hot that I had to take my shirt off. Trying to remain calm but showing appreciation for what he had done, I thanked him, and we continued to talk on the phone for about 10 minutes talking about how his day was going. As soon I got off the phone, I started screaming, jumped up from my chair, and started running up the basement stairs!! Before I made it to the top of the stairs, I felt a sharp pain in my big toe, but my excitement had me so distracted that it wasn't until I made it all the way to my bedroom that I realized that my toe was still hurting, unlike when I usually stub my toe and the pain would go away pretty fast. I fought through the pain and went to the grocery store to collect my money, dropped the money off at home, and since my toe was still hurting, I headed to the emergency room. As I had expected, I had fractured my big toe and had to use some of that money to cover my trip to the emergency room.

John and I would have good conversations. He taught me a lot about how to manage money, how to invest and how to get my own business started. After a few months, he retired, and our phone calls started slowing down. We communicated more through emails every few months. Later that year, I reached out to him. A week or so had gone by and I hadn't gotten a response. Sadly, I found out that he had passed away a month earlier. I'm so glad I had the pleasure of knowing John.

I work from home. I choose the hours and days that I want to work. I can take off any time I want for vacation, special events, sickness etc., and know that my job will be there when I'm ready to come back. My pay started at $18 an hour and has increased every year. I love the perks: don't have to drive in traffic or bad weather, can work in my pajamas or completely naked, no bosses standing over my shoulder or dealing with irritating co-workers. I make good money and I'm very popular because my voice sounds young for a 45-year-old.

When you have a job where you make good money and love what you do, a lot of times you want to talk about work with others. I was going around proud of what I do. Many of these men are lonely, don't have anyone to talk to and want some "safe" attention from a woman. Believe it or not, I often get calls where the customer doesn't necessarily want to talk about sex. Others couldn't understand why I would happily say " I'm A Phone Sex Operator" with a big smile on my face. Some would frown, look at me like I was crazy, or thought it was interesting, insisting they should do it too.

Being a phone sex operator is not as easy and exciting as most would think. The number one quality you must have is being open-minded. Men call you to talk about their fantasies and some of the things that excite and turn them on are illegal in the United States. No matter how nasty or disgusting their fantasies are, you must respond like you want to do the same things.

2.

What A Delivery!!!!

I had just put on my sexy short white sundress, the one with the low V cut and a soft flowing pleated bottom that barely reached my knees, when I hear the doorbell ring. By the time I get to the door, the UPS guy is just getting back into his truck and is about to pull off. I step outside to pick up this medium-sized package, and as I bend down to grab it, I feel the breeze come across the thin material of my purple lace thong, just as I hear the neighbor's screen door shut. I hurry inside, not daring to look back to see if he noticed that my ass was completely visible, and shut the door.

When I sit down on the couch, I giggle at the thought of my regular UPS delivery guy in my old neighborhood some years back. I had started a home-based business that dealt with health and beauty. A lot of our products helped people to better their health and lose weight, so I would get a lot of deliveries to my home. It was always the same guy.

Oh he was so sexy. We would chat a little while I searched for a pen because I always had to sign for it and he never had a pen on him, which I think he constantly did on purpose. He was tall and slender with well-kept dreads. I could tell he was from Louisiana because he would always say "Wazzam Miss," which always made me smile and feel a little tingling inside. A couple of times when I answered the door, hearing him talk made my nipples hard and he noticed. He would smile and talk for a few minutes longer. That's when I noticed his pretty teeth, nice smile. Once he did something with his tongue, nothing really perverted, but I did notice how long it was and how he flicked it with ease. During the warmer days when he came by with no jacket and just a snug fitting short sleeve shirt, I noticed his muscles and a few tattoos. I was always looking forward to my deliveries and us flirting back and forth. I think on several occasions I ordered products even when I didn't need them.

One year around my birthday, I was planning a beautiful 5-hour spa day and then the night out with my girls. As I was getting my clothes together for that evening and about to rush out and get me some nice heels, I heard the doorbell ring. It was a delivery!!!!! As this sexy man stood in my doorway again holding a package, smiling, glancing at my hard nipples poking thru my white sundress, similar to what I have on today, I asked him to step in while I found a pen. During our small talk, he wished me a Happy Birthday when he noticed the cards and balloons in the living room. Rushing and searching for this pen had me so flustered that I didn't noticed him undoing his pants. I finally found a pen on the windowsill above my kitchen sink. As I reached up on my tip toes to grab it, he came behind me and started kissing me on my neck, with his hard dick pressed up against me, and slid his hand up my dress and started rubbing my clit thru my panties.

His touch was gentle, and he smelled so intoxicating, my panties were getting wet so fast I didn't know how to react. Then he slid my panties to the side and pushed in his thick hard dick deep inside me. Mmmm those long strokes had me shaking when he started going harder and faster. I started cumming all over him. Then he pulled it out and squirted his hot cum on my ass cheeks. As I took a big exhale and tried to gather myself to say something, I turned around and he was gone. Left my package on the table. No Signature Needed!!!!!! The next week, I was back at it again, ordered my products, looking forward to the delivery. Then I realized that my birthday was the last time I would see him.

Mmmmm, I don't need to be reminiscing on this while in this dress on my way to my monthly spa day. My thong will be soaking wet if I don't hurry up and focus. I found a nice new spa that I want to try and don't want my first impression to be the girl with the pussy soaked panties. This relaxing massage is a much-needed stress reliever that I need after dealing with all types of irritating perverts today.

Heading to the spa, taking my time, giving my panties a chance to dry. As I walk in, I'm greeted at the counter with a glass of wine--my favorite, Pink Moscato. Then a woman leads me to this huge elegant bathroom decorated with 4 bouquets of tricolor roses, soft jazz playing, and my mineral bath water running. I start getting undressed while smelling all the roses and admiring this old-style home. Filling the tub almost to the drain, I step into this warm soothing water and soak for about 20 minutes. After taking my bath, I go to get my facial. The woman leads me into this small room and tells me to lie on my back on the massage bed and take off my glasses.

As she's massaging my face and head, she tells me about the history of this building. It's an old farm-style house that they converted into a spa. As she's talking with both hands massaging my head, we're both startled as her bracelets fly off the counter onto the floor. We kinda laugh it off as she continues with my facial. When she places the cucumbers on my eyes and a warm cloth over my face, she leaves the room. I hear her walk to the door, open the door as her voice traveled out while closing the door, and her footsteps slowly fade. About 3 minutes into me lying there in the room alone with my face covered, I feel a heavy presence floating above me. *I Feel Someone In The Room!!* I start praying and praying, "Lord please don't let whatever this is harm me, please lord make it go away please." About a minute later, she walks into the room, removes the towel and cucumbers off my face, and I jump up and get out of there quick, heading to my full body massage, Oh lord I really need it now!

As I'm lying on the massage table in just a purple thong, she starts massaging my neck, shoulders and back with the citrus aromatherapy oil. I'm in heaven. When she starts massaging my lower back and butt cheeks, I try not to squirm because my ass is one of my sensual spots. Then while rubbing on my lower back, she's pulling on my thong, making it press harder on my pussy. Then it was the thighs, most importantly my inner thighs. That oil, her soft hands, so close to my pussy, I am begging inside for her to rub up against my clit or stick her finger in me. I am able to keep my composure mainly because by now it's almost noon and my stomach is growling. Thank goodness they bring me lunch while I am getting my foot massage.

All that is left is my Mani Pedi. During my regular chit chat with other customers, I find out I'm not the only one experiencing strange things happening in the facial room. Out by 2, I am ready to get the weekend started.

3.

Call You WHAT!?

       Trying to get to know someone and build a relationship is impossible when the communication is 80% text, 20% conversation, even if they are so sexy that they make your mouth water and give you goose bumps just from the sound of their voice. No one shows me that more better than Anthony. I met him in the summer of last year at a coffee shop. I couldn't stop staring at him and he couldn't stop licking his lips and giving me that "I'm going to fuck the shit out of you" look. When he was standing at the counter making his order, I noticed he was bow-legged, about 5'9", mixed black and Cuban, muscular, and had juicy lips.

       We exchanged numbers and over the next two months, we tried to get to know each other, but our communication was off. When we talked on the phone, he would make jokes that were totally off topic. I understood him better in text, but you really can't get to know someone that way. You can't hear the expression in their voice. Are they saying it with a smile or are they mad? If what they are typing is really how they feel and speak or are they preparing a response that they think you want to hear? I really think that that was what Anthony was doing, typing the kind of response that is typical, not what he really felt.

One day we decide to meet for pizza at a place I've never been. It is more like an historical place with two levels of dining. The bar is on the first floor and Historical Events are scattered on the wall of the second floor. He gets there before I do, and it is a bit crowded. I walk in looking for him and immediately I'm approached by a drunk guy trying to force me to sit next to him at the bar. I'm looking around the room, even on the top level for him, but I don't see him anywhere. So I call him. When he answers, I ask him if he's upstairs on the second level. It is loud and that drunk guy is still trying to get me to sit down, so I step outside. Anthony says, "Second floor? there's no second floor. Hold up I'll come get you." He tells me to come around back. He comes out, we walk in where the floor goes slightly up, get to his table in the corner, sit down and Anthony picks the seat where the stairs are directly behind him while looking at me like I'm crazy, talking about there's no second floor.

The next four months, I get a "good morning" text every day and short texted conversations until he says he wants to see me again and invites me to his apartment. I put on a cute T-shirt dress, some sandals, and head over. Damn he is sexy as hell with all his clothes on. As we are watching a comedy, sipping on Moscato and eating pizza, I keep imagining him naked. We eventually make it to his bedroom where we start kissing and rubbing on each other. He gives me wet kisses from my titties down to my pussy. I feel those soft juicy lips all over my clit. He is sucking on it how I like. After I cum and he puts the condom on and slides into my pussy, he whispers in my ear, "Call me Daddy."

This is something that I don't usually do but since he isn't stroking it right, I figure this may help him get it right. I start saying, "Oh Daddy," "Fuck me hard Daddy." Then he starts cumming hard, rolls over and starts mumbling "5,4,3,2,1. What the hell have I just done."

Would you consider this "a compliment," "crazy," or "a red flag"? Listening to a friend after this happened, I took it as a compliment from someone who may be somewhat of an introvert.

After a few weeks, I arrange to see him again. Preparing for the night, I soak in a bubble bath, make sure my pussy is shaved smooth and soft. I start getting horny when I am rubbing in my sexy scented lotion, pack some sexy lingerie and some lube because his dick is thick with a fat head. I get there and after a little conversation, a glass of wine, and some comedy entertainment, I am ready!!! We start off kissing and rubbing on each other, me sucking on his dick and him eating my pussy. He slides it in. It feels so good UNTIL... He tells me he loves me. I moan. Then he says, "This is my pussy." I start moaning mmmmhhhhhhh. Then he says (in mid stroke), "If you cheat on me, I'll kill you."

What the fuck!!!!! My pussy instantly dries up!!!

I had planned to spend the night, so eventually he cums and I'm lying there, eyes wide open. It's 3 in the morning and he's falling asleep, holding me, so it is hard for me to slip out, get dressed and leave without him noticing and possibly going crazy on me. I barely close my eyes the rest of the night, but as soon as daylight hits, I get up and say, "I got to go, I have an early appointment." Trying to stay calm and not look like I'm scared, I get dressed, pack my shit, and head to the door. He opens the door for me and kisses me goodbye. Then he says, "Don't cheat on me, I will stab you to death," as he chuckles. I make it to my car, start it up, and pull off without putting my seat belt on. As soon as I make it out of the gated community, I thank the Lord I made it out safely. Thank goodness he doesn't know where I live. I blocked his calls and messages, yet every few months he calls me and leaves a message. I never listen to them. You have to be careful of who you put your sexual A game on because it may get deadly.

4.

The Secret Beach

It has been a warm, beautiful week in Tennessee when I get a Facebook invitation to a party Saturday at a secret beach at one of the state parks that I go to often. The day is perfect. 87 degrees with a slight breeze has me ready to get wet and have a little fun. I wear my royal blue tank top with the crisscross front low cut V-neck, showing lots of cleavage. The sides are long, but the front of my tank top only covers half of my blue multicolored short shorts which show off my smooth sexy long legs. I have on cute comfortable water shoes. I figured since I had never seen this secret beach before, we would have to do some walking to get there. I grab my teal one-piece swimsuit. The bottom is bikini cut, the top is a straight cut with spaghetti thin straps that has a sheer cover up attached that can be crisscrossed and tied behind the neck, and the bottom is like a short skirt that just barely covers my little round ass. I grab a towel and a 4 pack of the miniature Moscato wine.

We get to the meeting spot and are given a map with instructions. At that time, it is 3 of us that head out on the dirt path. During this 20-minute walk, the pavement goes from a wide rocky road to a dirt road, then to a more narrow semi grassy path. We pass a lighthouse and a few plaques that give informative facts about this area of the park. When we finally arrive, only 4 people are there and a family with their dog, that keeps running into the water to catch the ball his family is throwing. As more people arrive including the host with music and food, it becomes a party!

It is going nice. I am prepared to see some topless, sexy fun, you know the kind you get with the "majority race" when it comes to alcoholic drinks, skimpy bikinis and being by the water. I am a little disappointed that none of that is happening until I see a tall, thick, almond brown man with a sexy smile walk up. Oh am I happy to see him! Deon works in finance and lives in the downtown area near the park. As we are talking, the combination of his slightly deep voice, pretty white teeth, sexy smile, and him putting his soft hands on my arm as we talk has my pussy throbbing.

We continue to chit chat, flirt a little bit and talk about getting in the water. I tell him I will if he will. He hadn't brought his swim trunks and mine are in my bag with no bathroom in sight to go change. Deon tells me he'll go get his and he'll cover me while I change into mine. I only say I will do that because I don't think he is going to come back, being that it's a long walk back to the car and a 10-minute drive to get out of the park. Sitting there watching people interacting with each other, one lady playing a steel pan drum, others swimming in the water, I start thinking and getting nervous. What if he does come back! I don't want him to see me naked. I ask one of the ladies if she will follow me into the woods and hold her towel up so I can change into my swimsuit. She does. I put my shorts and tank top back on over my swimsuit and sit down in my lawn chair waiting to see if Deon comes back. About 10 minutes later, here he comes with swim shorts in his hand. He is a little disappointed when I tell him I have already changed, and he slides my shorts down and takes my tank top off. He asks me to hold his towel up while he changes into his trunks. We go into the woods and I tell him, "I won't look."

He says, "You can look, I'm not embarrassed."

It is hard for me not to look being that I am trying to keep him covered with a towel that is only twice the size of a big washcloth. I am impressed to see that his dick is thick and 7 inches long, soft. He tells me to grab it, I take my hand and wrap it around his dick and stroke it back and forth about three times and then force myself to stop because it is getting hard and there is a lot of activity going on around us. We go into the water for a while, have some drinks, enjoying the event and each other's company.

As time goes by and some people are starting to leave, we relax at our spot and listen to this lady play her drum. Deon is sitting in my chair and I'm standing in front of him, and as we're talking, he notices my nipples are hard. He slides his finger across the front of my swimsuit right across my clit, and again my pussy starts throbbing. There are people around and close by, which really turns me on, but since my swimsuit has a little skirt type cover up over the bottom of it, it is hard to see him touching me. I stand there trying to have a regular conversation while he slides his finger under my swimsuit and rubs his soft fingers on my clit. My pussy gets so wet so fast. The more I try to hide my excitement while looking around at others, trying to have a conversation and trying to look inconspicuous, the more I get turned on, my pussy gets wetter, my body starts trembling with pleasure. Deon is rubbing my pussy for about ten minutes, all the while I'm telling him he better stop before I take him in the woods and fuck him right then and there. He doesn't stop...

A few minutes later I grab his hand and lead him out into the woods. The trees are thick in some areas and some spots have wide open areas. When I find a spot that I think is just right, I turn around and start kissing him. He takes my swimsuit completely off and gets down on his knees and starts licking and sucking on my soaked pussy. As I look around, I don't see anyone but their voices sound so close by that the thought of someone watching us and the feel of a tongue from a sexy man that I just met makes me cum so hard, I have to cover my mouth to prevent me from moaning too loud. Without hesitation I squat down and take his thick, hard nine and a half inches in my mouth and suck it like I have a cherry popsicle in my mouth, and I am thirsty. I am slobbering all over his dick, taking it deeper and deeper into my mouth. Running my tongue around the rim and across his pee hole. I feel him starting to swell up in my mouth. Then he reaches down and pulls me up, turns me around and bends me over and slides right into my wet and ready waiting pussy. Oh he feels so good inside of me!! He's long stroking my pussy and squeezing one titty while pinching my nipple on the other one, and I start cumming again. Shortly after, he pulls his dick out and squirts his cum on the grass.

We get dressed, gather our composure, kiss, and head back to our spot on the beach. It appears no one had noticed we left, so we eat some BBQ, chat a little more, exchange numbers and head back to our cars.

Over the next few days, we talk, text, and send each other sexy pics. Oh, this man has me wanting more. He is perfect since he really brings out the exhibitionist in me, loving public sex. Our next adventure is at a hot tub spa. We meet at the spa on a Friday afternoon around 3 pm. As we are going in and he's paying for our spa time and drinks, I'm standing there horny as hell but trying to look innocent, so I won't give the cashier any idea that we are just going in there to fuck. We go in our hot tub room, which was decorated like a garden, with a shower to the right, next to a padded bench with pillows and a mirror above. The hot tub area was a step down from the changing area and you had your choice of music, level of jet flow and temperature. Immediately we start kissing and undressing, he's rubbing my pussy and sucking on my nipple, I'm stroking on his dick as it's getting harder and my pussy getting wet. He goes down and starts licking and sucking on my clit as he slides his finger into my pussy as I'm trying again not to moan too loud as I am squirting my cum in his face.

The first time we met I was controlled by my body's overwhelming desire to fuck him outside and threw all caution to the wind by not using a condom, I am prepared to use one today. I bring a Magnum and a Trojan extra-large condom. The problem is the Trojan condom is too tight and the Magnum condom won't go all the way down, so once again he is going in me raw. Besides praying that he doesn't have any STD's, my concern is I know when I have sex without a condom, I catch feelings. I don't want to have that experience by myself.

We do it on the bench, but after a while it gets uncomfortable because he is banging me so hard. So we do it in the hot tub. He sits down on the step in the tub and I straddle him, guiding his dick in me as I slide down on it. Because I'm so lightweight in the water, he grabs my waist and starts slamming me down on his dick. Then I get on my knees on the step and he slides in from the back, holding my waist and pounding in my pussy. Then we get the ten-minute warning. We know we have to get cleaned up and out of there, but our passion is so strong. We even do it again in the shower.
Once again I put on that innocent look as I walk from the room, out to the lobby and then to my car. I am so relaxed and have a huge smile on my face on my ride home.

Over the summer, we texted and sexted a lot but our busy schedules never allowed us to meet up until one chilly day in December, he sends me a pic of his dick and text saying "Cum and check out the balcony view." I am there an hour and a half later. He greets me at the front door of his apartment building and the sexual tension starts building. We get in the elevator headed to the 18th floor to his apartment, and he grabs my hand and puts in down his jogging pants. Feeling his dick in my hand brings back wonderful memories. We almost get caught when the doors start opening and a guy is standing there, and my hands are still in his pants. Luckily, I let go and pull my hand out before the door opens all the way. We step out and head to the right, going down the hall to his apartment. Passing a few apartments and getting to the end of that hall, we make another right and his apartment is the third one down, second one from the other end.

We step in. I put my purse down on the small table next to a bench, across from the coat closet. He takes my coat and hangs it up while I sit on the bench and take off my boots. When I stand up, he grabs me close and starts kissing and undressing me right in front of his open apartment door. He takes off his clothes and bends me over and slides that big hard dick inside my pussy. I am LOVING IT!!!!!! While he's fucking me right there, I hear people walking down the halls, going in and out of different apartments. I cum all on his dick.

We finally get into his bed. He licks and sucks me from head to toe. We do a 69 and I slobber all on his dick but when he gets on top of me and holds my legs back, that's when I know for sure his dick is bigger than I originally thought. It feels amazing feeling his body pressed up against mine, feeling him kissing me and sliding in and out of me at the same time. I'm thinking, oh this is the best sex I've had in a while, as we squirt at the same time, me all on his dick and him squirting cum all in my pussy.

5.

Don't Put Me in Your Shit

I'm so busy, working hard, handling my day to day activities when I realize 3 months have gone by. Talking dirty to all these men, has me so horny that I call up an old friend. Haven't seen him in about 7 months. I am reminiscing about how good it was the last time. Good dick will make you get all bundled up and drive in the cold on wet and slippery dark roads, especially when you have the plans to spend the night, knowing you will experience that good orgasmic pleasure at least 3 times before its time to go.

The first one is amazing, lasting about an hour. The second time is great also even though it doesn't last as long, but both times have me begging him to cum because I am trembling out of control from cumming so much. As I am finally falling asleep, I'm thinking about how good that morning sex is going to be.

Instead, I am awakened, startled by a loud banging on the front door of his apartment. Looking at me in a panic, with his finger to his lips, he tells me to be quiet and don't move. I'm lying there in his bed, totally naked, listening to the banging getting harder and louder, and hearing a woman calling out his name at 4:30 in the morning, while he's in his underwear pacing back and forth, mumbling about "what is she doing here," "no she didn't just pop up on me like that," trying to assure me that they are just childhood friends and he's single. The banging gets so loud that I think she is going to bust the door open. Every time I try to sit up, he's telling me not to move. By now he's almost fully dressed, practicing his lies out loud, pacing back and forth, peeking out the bedroom window, while trying to keep the light that's coming off his cell phone covered, while trying to check his voice mail. I'm looking at this man like *No this punk ass didn't put me in this situation*, as I'm listening to him practice his lies, call his son to back up his lies, and getting mad that this chick caught him, while I'm praying that I make it out of there alive.

After about 30 minutes of him waiting to make sure she's gone, he goes in the living room to grab my clothes and tells me that he wants me to drop him off at his son's house. I put my top and leggings on, probably backwards because we're still in the dark, grab my panties and bra and put them in my purse, put my crossbody purse on under my coat, slide my boots on and tell him I'm going to go warm up the car while he's putting the condom wrappers in the trash bag to take out to the dumpster. I walk out the door with my keys in one hand and my mace in the other, get in the car and take off!! Left him there to deal with his own drama. *Don't put me in your shit!*

The next day he texts me asking how I am doing and saying he's got things cleared up!!! That text gets no response, just like a few more he sent weeks after.

They say nowadays when you ask a man if he's single, you also have to ask if there is a woman out there that *thinks you're her man*. I believe it now. Being sexually free and safe shouldn't come with drama. That just takes all the fun out of it.